Dedicated to all who have been touched
by the magic of loving a doll.

Dedications

This book is dedicated to the real doll lady,
Dorothy D. Fogelberg, great aunt and family friend.

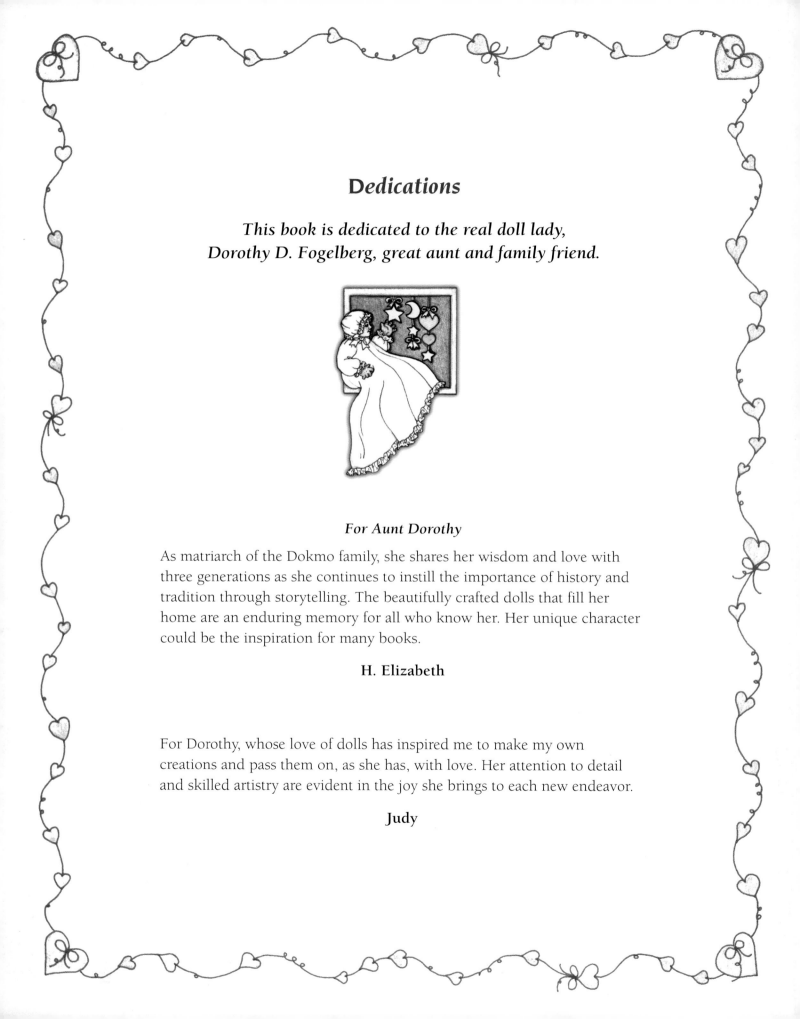

For Aunt Dorothy

As matriarch of the Dokmo family, she shares her wisdom and love with three generations as she continues to instill the importance of history and tradition through storytelling. The beautifully crafted dolls that fill her home are an enduring memory for all who know her. Her unique character could be the inspiration for many books.

H. Elizabeth

For Dorothy, whose love of dolls has inspired me to make my own creations and pass them on, as she has, with love. Her attention to detail and skilled artistry are evident in the joy she brings to each new endeavor.

Judy

Hidden within the pure hearts of the young
and the distant memories of the old
is a secret truth.
This magical wisdom is passed
from generation to generation
by gentle souls who softly whisper,
"Treat them kindly and with great love,
for dolls are just like people."

Once, many years ago,
I received a gift of great
meaning – a gift I have
always treasured. And
now, my precious one,
with this doll, I pass the
story on to you...

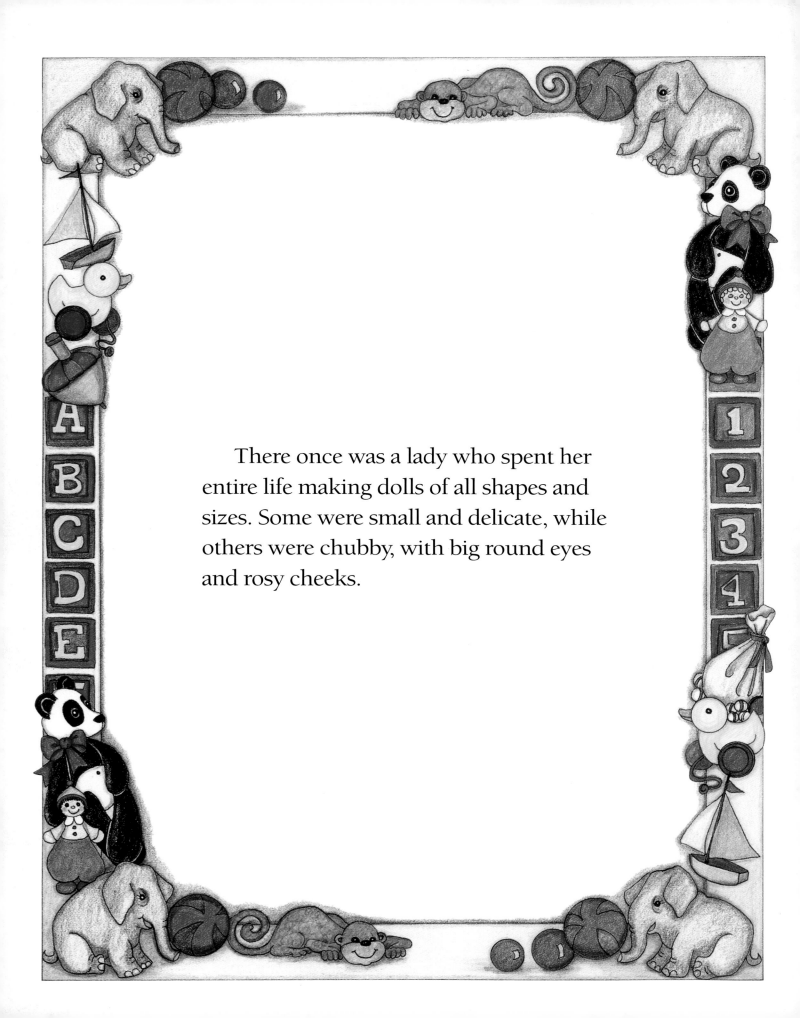

There once was a lady who spent her entire life making dolls of all shapes and sizes. Some were small and delicate, while others were chubby, with big round eyes and rosy cheeks.

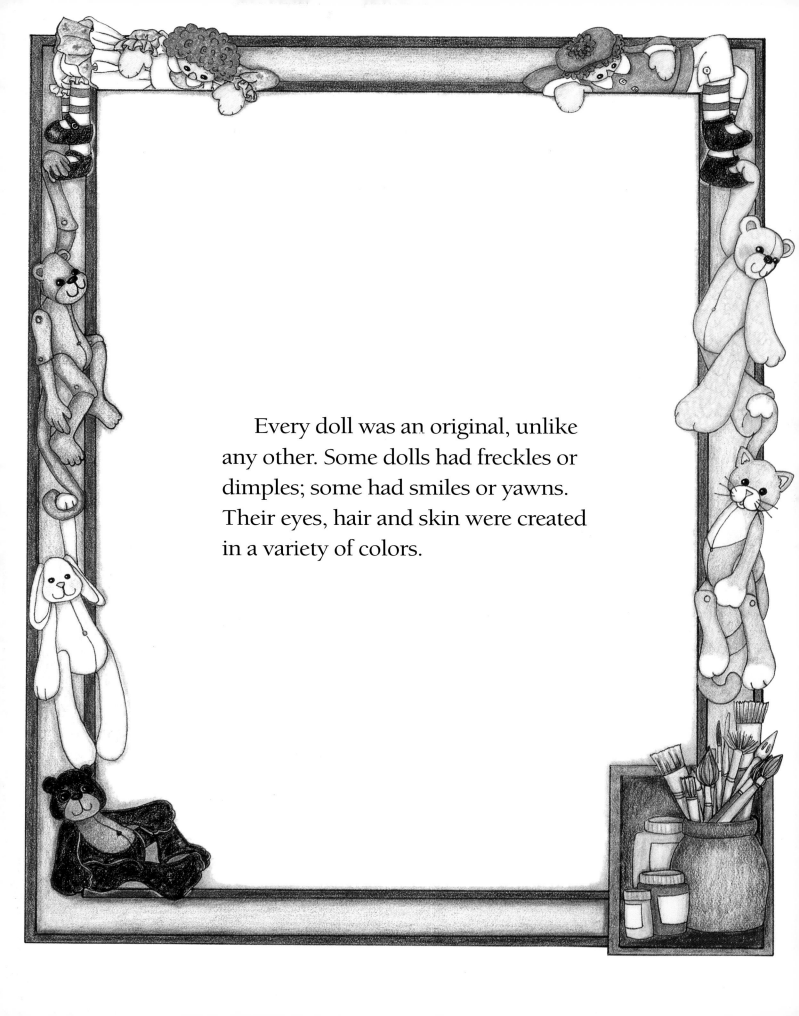

Every doll was an original, unlike any other. Some dolls had freckles or dimples; some had smiles or yawns. Their eyes, hair and skin were created in a variety of colors.

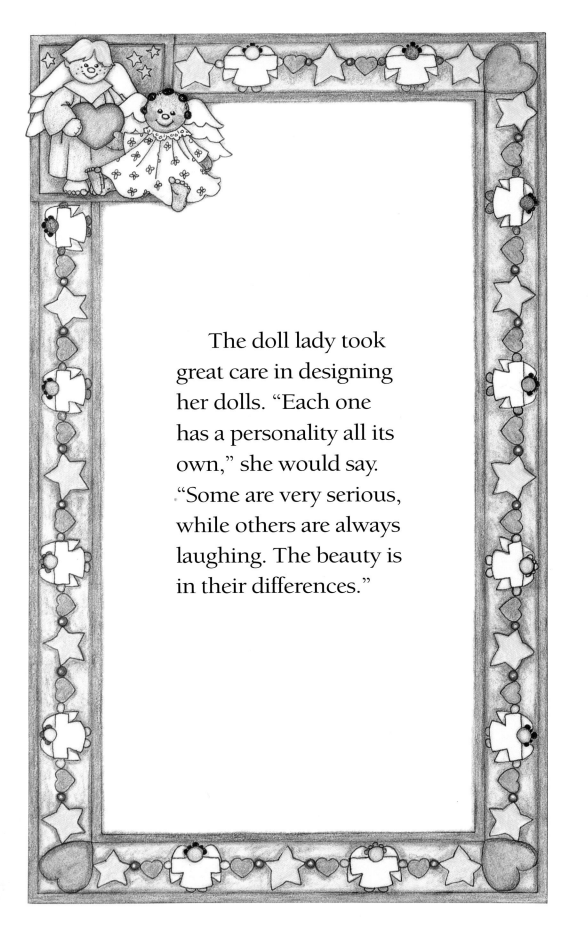

The doll lady took
great care in designing
her dolls. "Each one
has a personality all its
own," she would say.
"Some are very serious,
while others are always
laughing. The beauty is
in their differences."

As the kind woman gave her dolls to little boys and girls, she would say, "Take very special care of your doll, for dolls are just like people. They need to be well loved, held tenderly and always respected for their uniqueness."

The doll lady said this because she knew a secret truth –
that when you are young, you learn how to treat others. Those
who are shown love and respect as children will know how to

be loving and caring as they grow older.
Love is like a seed that must be planted
and cared for in order to grow.

This wise woman loved all children just as she loved her dolls. On her daily walks she would reach out and gently touch a child's head, telling the parents, "Give him a doll; he will learn to be kind," or "give her a doll; it will help her to express love."

As the years passed, the doll lady could no longer make as many dolls as when she was younger. Her hands worked more slowly, but always with the same love and skill. She still treasured every doll as if it were her own child.

One day, when she had become quite old, the doll lady went around her neighborhood giving away all her dolls, until none were left. As she placed each doll in a child's arms, she would whisper, "Take very special care of your doll, for dolls are just like people. They need to be well loved, held tenderly and always respected for their uniqueness."

Though many
years have passed,
the doll lady is still
fondly remembered.
Those of us who
received her dolls
when we were
young are now
grownup and have
children of our own.
It is our turn to pass
along the secret
truth she taught
us so long ago.

Someday, my little one, when
you place a doll into the arms
of your own child, you too will
begin to tell the story, "There was
once a doll lady…"

The HeartStrings Collection

Enchanting Children's Picture Books

Written by H. Elizabeth Collins-Varni
Illustrated by Judy Kuusisto

To Sleep with the Angels

To Sleep with the Angels is the heartwarming story of a young girl who spends her nights flying on magical adventures with her Guardian Angel. This gentle, comforting book reassures children at bedtime and encourages them to call upon their own special angels. A finalist for **Best Children's Book of 2000** awarded by the Coalition of Visionary Retailers, it has become a nighttime favorite for parents and children.

The Doll Lady

There once was a woman who spent her entire life creating remarkable dolls for children. "Treat them kindly and with great love," she would say, "for dolls are just like people." New generations continue to pass on this enduring message whenever they give the precious gift of a doll.

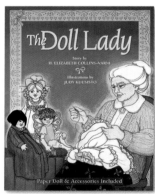

Planting Memories
(A 2002 release)

This delightful book tells the story of a glorious garden filled with flowers in every color of the rainbow. Each plant holds the memory of a special person who has touched the gardener's life. The exquisite illustrations reflect Judy's love of flowers, and Elizabeth's tender story will touch every heart.

THE ILLUMINATION ARTS COLLECTION OF INSPIRING CHILDREN'S BOOKS

THE LITTLE WIZARD
Written and Illustrated by Jody Bergsma $15.95   0-935699-19-8
A young boy discovers a wizard's cloak while on a mission to save his mother's life.

WINGS OF CHANGE
By Franklin Hill, Ph.D., illlustrated by Aries Cheung $15.95   0-935699-18-X
A happy little caterpillar resists his approaching transformation into a butterfly.

ALL I SEE IS PART OF ME
Winner – 1996 Award of Excellence from Body Mind Spirit Magazine
By Chara Curtis, illustrated by Cynthia Aldrich $15.95   0-935699-07-4
In this international bestseller, a child finds the light within his heart and his common link with all of life.

THE BONSAI BEAR
Finalist – 2000 Visionary Award for Best Children's Book – Coalition of Visionary Retailers
By Bernard Libster, illustrated by Aries Cheung $15.95   0-935699-15-5
Issa uses bonsai methods to keep his pet bear small, but the playful cub dreams of following his true nature.

CORNELIUS AND THE DOG STAR
Winner – 1996 Award of Excellence from Body Mind Spirit Magazine
By Diana Spyropulos, illustrated by Ray Williams $15.95   0-935699-08-2
Grouchy old Cornelius Basset Hound can't enter Dog Heaven until he learns about love, fun, and kindness.

DRAGON
Winner – 2000 Visionary Award for Best Children's Book – Coalition of Visionary Retailers
Written and Illustrated by Jody Bergsma $15.95   0-935699-17-1
Born on the same day, a gentle prince and a fire-breathing dragon share a prophetic destiny.

DREAMBIRDS
Winner – 1998 Visionary Award for Best Children's Book – Coalition of Visionary Retailers
By David Ogden, illustrated by Jody Bergsma $16.95   0-935699-09-0
A Native American boy battles his own ego as he searches for the elusive dreambird and its powerful gift.

FUN IS A FEELING
By Chara M. Curtis, illustrated by Cynthia Aldrich $15.95   0-935699-13-9
Find your fun! "Fun isn't something or somewhere or who. It's a feeling of joy that lives inside of you."

HOW FAR TO HEAVEN?
By Chara M. Curtis, illustrated by Cynthia Aldrich $15.95   0-935699-06-6
Exploring the wonders of nature, Nanna and her granddaughter discover heaven all around them.

THE RIGHT TOUCH
Winner – Benjamin Franklin Parenting Award, Selected as Outstanding by the Parents Council
By Sandy Kleven, LCSW, illustrated by Jody Bergsma $15.95   0-935699-10-4
This beautifully illustrated read-aloud story teaches children how to prevent sexual abuse.

SKY CASTLE
"Children's Choice for 1999" by Children's Book Council
By Sandra Hanken, illustrated by Jody Bergsma $15.95   0-935699-14-7
Alive with dolphins, parrots and fairies, this magical tale inspires us to believe in the power of our dreams.

TO SLEEP WITH THE ANGELS
Finalist – 2000 Visionary Award for Best Children's Book – Coalition of Visionary Retailers
By H. Elizabeth Collins, illustrated by Judy Kuusisto $15.95   0-935699-16-3
A young girl's guardian Angel comforts her to sleep, filling her dreams with magical adventures.

✿ ✿ ✿ ✿ ✿ ✿

Direct U.S. Orders: add $2.00 postage; each additional book add $1.00. Free shipping with 5 or more books.

ILLUMINATION ARTS PUBLISHING COMPANY
P.O. Box 1865, Bellevue, WA 98009 ✿ 1.888.210.8216 ✿ 425.644.7185 ✿ fax: 425.644.9274
E-mail: liteinfo@illumin.com ✿ www.illumin.com

"Each day at the Museum of Doll Art we see in 'grown-ups' the positive influence that dolls have in children's lives. Many of us have known that loving and caring for a doll prepare us for life. This beautiful book relates the story of a dollmaker who brings that valuable message to the many children whose lives she touches. Based on the life of a real dollmaker, *The Doll Lady* lovingly reveals the true purpose of dolls, exploring the thin line between dolls and real people. Elizabeth Collins-Varni and Judy Kuusisto have captured these special feelings for us to carry in our hearts."

Rosalie Whyel
Director, Rosalie Whyel Museum of Doll Art
Bellevue, Washington
Member NIADA, UFDC, NADDA

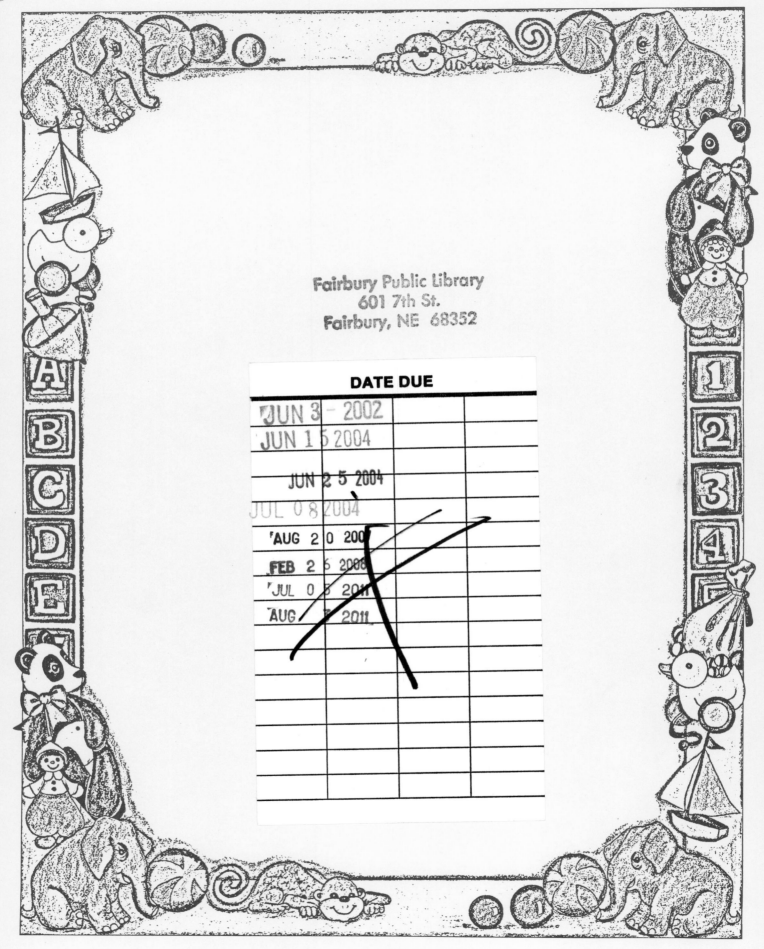